Dear Parents:

Congratulations! Your child is taking the first steps on an exciting journey. The destination? Independent reading!

STEP INTO READING® will help your child get there. The program offers five steps to reading success. Each step includes fun stories and colorful art or photographs. In addition to original fiction and books with favorite characters, there are Step into Reading Non-Fiction Readers, Phonics Readers and Boxed Sets, Sticker Readers, and Comic Readers—a complete literacy program with something to interest every child.

Learning to Read, Step by Step!

Ready to Read   Preschool–Kindergarten
• big type and easy words • rhyme and rhythm • picture clues
For children who know the alphabet and are eager to begin reading.

Reading with Help   Preschool–Grade 1
• basic vocabulary • short sentences • simple stories
For children who recognize familiar words and sound out new words with help.

Reading on Your Own   Grades 1–3
• engaging characters • easy-to-follow plots • popular topics
For children who are ready to read on their own.

Reading Paragraphs   Grades 2–3
• challenging vocabulary • short paragraphs • exciting stories
For newly independent readers who read simple sentences with confidence.

Ready for Chapters   Grades 2–4
• chapters • longer paragraphs • full-color art
For children who want to take the plunge into chapter books but still like colorful pictures.

STEP INTO READING® is designed to give every child a successful reading experience. The grade levels are only guides; children will progress through the steps at their own speed, developing confidence in their reading.

Remember, a lifetime love of reading starts with a single step!

Special thanks to Charnita Belcher, Ryan Ferguson, Kristine Lombardi, Sammie Suchland, Debra Mostow Zakarin, Christopher Keenan, Shannon Nettleton, Ann Austen, Susan Corbin, Rachael Datello, Gabrielle Hill, Renata Marchand, Grant Moran, Julia Pistor, Jaya Ramdath, Renevee Romero-Villegas, Garrett Sander, Sarah Serata, Teale Sperling, and Mainframe Studios

Published in the United States by Random House Children's Books, a division of Penguin Random House LLC, 1745 Broadway, New York, NY 10019, and in Canada by Penguin Random House Canada Limited, Toronto.

Step into Reading, Random House, and the Random House colophon are registered trademarks of Penguin Random House LLC.

Visit us on the Web!
StepIntoReading.com
rhcbooks.com

Educators and librarians, for a variety of teaching tools, visit us at RHTeachersLibrarians.com

ISBN 978-1-5247-6908-6 (trade) — ISBN 978-1-5247-6909-3 (lib. bdg.)

Printed in the United States of America
10 9 8 7 6 5 4 3 2 1

Barbie
dreamhouse adventures

The
Great
Cake Race

adapted by Kristen L. Depken
based on the original screenplay
by Grant Moran

Random House 🏠 New York

Barbie and her sisters
play with their puppies.
Stacie has news.

She has entered Barbie
in the great cake race!
It will be on TV.
Barbie will bake and race!

Stacie will be
Barbie's coach.
They train
on a trampoline.

Barbie walks
on a tightrope.
She holds a tray
of cupcakes.

The day of the race,
Barbie meets Tammy.
They will race
against each other.

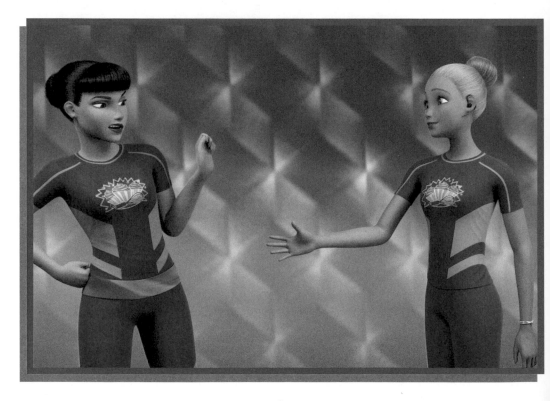

First,
they must climb
a rock wall.
Giant oven mitts try
to push Barbie off.

Barbie's sisters
cheer for her.

Barbie makes it
to the top!

Next,
the girls must get eggs
from a giant chicken.

Tammy has two eggs.

She takes the lead!

Barbie leaps!

She slides down a rope

and catches up.

Now both girls must
bring sugar to the top
of a giant cake.
Tammy is already there.
She is cheating!

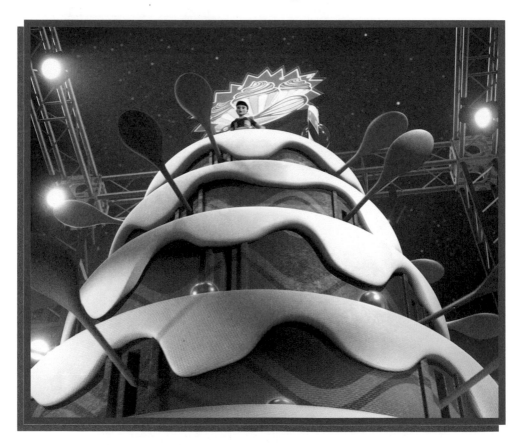

Barbie's sisters
are mad that Tammy
is cheating.
They tell Barbie
to quit.

Barbie will not give up.

She has an idea.

She flings her sugar
to the top of the cake.
She is still
in the race!

It is time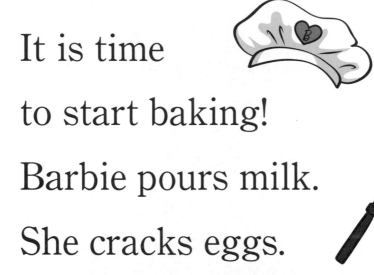
to start baking!
Barbie pours milk.
She cracks eggs.

Tammy pours milk.

She stirs.

She is worried

that Barbie will win.

The cupcakes are baking.
Suddenly,
the girls rise
into the air.

There is a surprise event.
It is an icing
tug-of-war!

Barbie tugs the rope.

Tammy cheats again.

She flings a spider

at Barbie.

Barbie tosses

the spider away.

It lands on Tammy.

Tammy falls.

She is out of the race!

Barbie ices her cupcakes

just in time.

Barbie wins
the great cake race!
Hooray!